A Very Naughty Little Girl

GOES CAMPING

(the Jennifer and Sarah series 2)

By

Abigail Strauss

Illustrations by Su Novis
(with a contribution of drawings by the children in the story)

Grosvenor House
Publishing Limited

This book is published by
Grosvenor House Publishing Ltd
Link House
140 The Broadway, Tolworth, Surrey, KT6 7HT.
www.grosvenorhousepublishing.co.uk

A CIP record for this book
is available from the British Library

Paperback ISBN 978-1-83975-952-9
Hardback ISBN 978-1-83975-953-6
Ebook ISBN 978-1-83975-954-3

ACKNOWLEDGEMENTS

This book would not have been possible without the invaluable support and encouragement of my sister and best friend, Julie. Her enthusiasm inspired me to write this book, for which I will be eternally grateful.

My gratitude also goes to my lifelong friend, Su Novis, whose charming illustrations have brought my book to life.

1. Preparing for the Camping Holiday

Best friends, Jennifer and Sarah, had broken up from school for the summer holidays and there was much excitement as the families were going camping together.

Sarah was now a little older since her last adventure so she was not so naughty (we hope!) It would be her seventh birthday whilst she was on holiday and her mother, Danielle, was planning a party for her with a few surprises.

The two families, plus Rusty, the dog, all met to discuss what they would need for this ten-day holiday.

"Now then," said Jennifer's daddy, Charlie, clapping his hands. "Isn't this exciting?!"

"Yesss!" everyone shouted.

Charlie continued, "but we need to make a plan so that everything runs smoothly."

Sarah's daddy said, "I think we should carry all the cooking equipment in our car because you will be taking two tents and, of course, Rusty."

Jennifer's Mummy, Vicky, said, "Danielle and I will share the food and other bits and bobs needed for cooking, etc."

Danielle whispered to Vicky, "I will bring the party food," and Vicky whispered back that she would bring the birthday cake.

Lee put up his hand and said, "Can we take the rounders set?"

"Yes, of course," replied Sarah's daddy, "and you can all take a small rucksack with your own choice of games; and don't forget to pack your swimsuits as the campsite is near the seaside so we will be going to the beach for a picnic."

2. Exploring the Campsite and First Night in the Tents

At last the day arrived to start the camping holiday and there was much activity at both homes as they packed their cars. Then they were off - the journey to the campsite would take about one hour.

On arrival at the site, the two dads parked up beside the campsite office to book them in.

A place had been reserved for them so that their tents were next to each other.

Everyone lent a hand in unloading the cars and erecting the tents. Eventually, they all flopped down on the grass and breathed a sigh of relief - the tents were in position and everything in its place.

"Can we go and explore now?" asked Nick, as all the children jumped to their feet.

"Have a glass of orange juice before you go, you must all be thirsty after your hard work," said Vicky.

As the children scampered off, closely followed by Rusty, the mums and dads relaxed for a while and then set up the stove to boil the kettle for cups of tea.

Vicky said, "Let's make this a holiday to remember!"

It was a large campsite and as the friends wandered around, they were amazed to see so many tents.

"Look," cried Mat, "there's a farm over there!" and sure enough there were all sorts of animals in the farmyard which was on the edge of the campsite and they could see a mother pig with her piglets, a cow, looking over the fence and some horses.

As they carried on walking around the edge of the campsite they came across a large enclosed area covered in netting. As they drew nearer there was a large collection of brightly coloured butterflies fluttering about. The children gasped with delight at the scene, and later discovered that the area was a butterfly sanctuary where they were protected.

Later that day, the children were all tired after their exciting first day and so, after a supper of fish and chips from the local takeaway, they crawled into their camp beds and were soon fast asleep. The mums and dads sat chatting by the tents for a while and then they joined the children.

Sarah and her mummy and daddy in one tent and her four brothers in another, which had been given to them by their Grandparents and, although it was old and still in good condition, it looked out of place amongst all the other modern tents.

Jennifer shared her parents' tent. She tossed and turned and then sat up and realised what was wrong – her favourite teddy bears, Daisy and Henry, were still in her rucksack. She grabbed them both and snuggled back down in her sleeping bag.

3. Getting Ready for Sarah's Birthday Party

The next day was Sarah's birthday and there was much to do preparing for her party. After breakfast Sarah opened her birthday presents and thanked everyone - her parents had given her a lovely new party dress which was a pretty pink with matching shoes.

Vicky said: "Now, there is a lot to do before the party so everyone will have a job to do, except the birthday girl!" Danielle suggested Sarah should visit the farmyard and butterflies, with one of her brothers for company.

"I'll go," said Mat, so they trotted off happily while everyone else set about their tasks. Jennifer was in charge of blowing up balloons and tying a piece of string to each one so they could all be attached to a chair to stop them blowing away in the wind. Sarah's eldest brother, Zane, had wrapped up a toy to play 'Pass the Parcel' and was busy finding some suitable music on his phone to play during the game.

The dads set up the picnic tables for the party food and the folding chairs, which they arranged in a circle for the adults. A large picnic blanket was also spread on the grass for the children to sit on – luckily the weather was glorious so the ground was dry.

"Oh, no", shrieked Danielle, "I've forgotten the candles for the cake!"

"Don't worry," said Nick, "I'll run over to the camp shop – I'm sure they'll have some." They all waited anxiously for his return and soon he was running back with his arms in the air which meant he had been successful!

4. The Collapsing Tent and an Exciting Discovery

On the way back from her walk with Mat, Sarah spotted something sparkling on the grass, so she bent down to investigate and found a beautiful diamond ring!

"Gosh, look how it catches the sunlight, glittering with all the colours of the rainbow," exclaimed Mat.

"I shall hand it into the campsite office when we get back – whoever has lost this must be heartbroken," said Sarah, pushing the ring firmly into her pocket for safety.

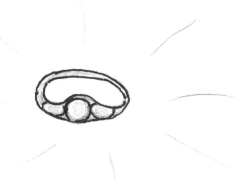

They continued walking back to their camp and on the way passed a small tent that sounded as though it contained a group of children because they heard them giggling and shouting excitedly. Eager to find out what they were playing and to say, "Hello," Sarah walked round to the front of the tent but the tent flap was closed so she went round to the back.

Mat said, "I'll go back now and help the others – don't be too long."

Sarah lifted the edge of the canvas and decided to crawl in, (bad idea!) She started to crawl under the canvass and almost succeeded when disaster struck! Her shoe caught on the framework that kept the tent upright, and gradually it began to collapse! Sarah was terrified and quickly slithered backwards out of the tent. There was chaos as the children were shrieking, laughing and crying, which alerted the surrounding campers who rushed to their aid.

Sarah ran back to her camp crying, "Mummy, Mummy, it was an accident – I didn't mean to do it!" Jennifer heard her friend's distress and rushed to meet her.

"What's happened? Calm down and tell me slowly," she said, soothingly, as Sarah continued to sob.

Sarah's daddy also heard his daughter's cries and ran to put his arms around her. When at last Sarah stopped sobbing she told them the whole story and said again that she had not meant any harm to those children in the tent.

Her daddy said, "As you have owned up to this catastrophe, you are no longer 'A VERY NAUGHTY LITTLE GIRL' (we hope!) and I think you and I should go and apologise to the parents." So he took her hand and they walked back to the scene where the accident happened.

On the way back to their camp, Sarah suddenly remembered the ring and felt in her pocket – yes, thankfully, it was still there so she explained to her daddy where she found it. He said that the ring must be handed in to the campsite office so they went there immediately.

5. Birthday Party Surprises

The birthday party was about to begin. Sarah had changed into her new party dress and Jennifer looked pretty in her bright blue party dress.

Suddenly, Lee pointed to the entrance of the campsite and shouted, "I know those three people!"

Everyone looked across the field and Sarah cried, "Oh, oh, it's Grandma Janet and Grandad Geoff, and they're with Grandad Brian!" and fled across the grass to greet them.

She threw her arms around her Grandma, who smothered her in kisses, and then Sarah grabbed Grandpa Geoff, nearly knocking him over!

Grandad Brian lifted his granddaughter into a huge hug, saying that he wouldn't have missed her birthday party for the world.

6. More surprises for Sarah

There was another surprise in store for Sarah! As everyone was chatting and enjoying cold drinks on this lovely sunny day, Mat jumped up from the blanket and shouted that there were four girls looking lost at the campsite entrance.

"They are my school friends!" yelled Sarah and raced over to meet them. "What a lovely surprise," she said, hugging them all in turn.

Justine, Thea, Isabella and Maya walked back to the camp with Sarah, chattering excitedly, saying that they had been looking forward to this for ages. Their parents had dropped them off and would be coming back to collect them later.

7. Party Games and Birthday Presents

While Vicky and Danielle set out the party food, Charlie organised a game of rounders for the children, who enjoyed it so much they didn't want to stop and Rusty raced around obviously thinking the game was just for him!

Everyone tucked into the delicious party food which consisted of chicken drumsticks, sausage rolls, cheese straws, Scotch eggs (a hard-boiled egg coated in sausage meat) which were yummy! There was also a choice of sandwiches.

For dessert there were strawberries, ice cream and meringues, together with a tray of individual raspberry and lime jellies.

After the picnic the children sat in a circle on the blanket and Grandad Geoff presented a small parcel to Sarah and said, "Grandma and I hope you like it!" Sarah was delighted when she opened the box and found a pretty silver bracelet inside.

Isabella also gave Sarah a present and said, "With love from your school friends - we can't wait to play it with you!" The gift was a game of Junior Scrabble, which pleased Sarah as she loved word games.

Then it was Grandad Brian's turn, who also gave Sarah a small parcel. When she opened it she was thrilled to find a lovely silver necklace that matched perfectly with her bracelet!

Jennifer said, "There's just one more surprise," and gave Sarah a gift from her neighbours, Maisie-Jean, her piano teacher, and Julie, a good friend who owned a parrot that talked! The two neighbours had known Sarah ever since she and Jennifer became best friends.

"Oh, how lovely!" exclaimed Sarah, holding up a pretty little trinket box that played a tune when the lid was opened.

"What a coincidence," cried Jennifer, "that's the same piece of music I'm learning in my piano lessons at the moment – 'Fur Elise' by the wonderful composer, Ludwig Van Beethoven."

8. Birthday Cake and Balloons

It was nearly time for Sarah's guests to go home so Nick suggested they play one more game.

Zane said, "How about 'Pass the Parcel'?" and the children chorused "Yes please!" He pulled out the parcel he'd prepared from his rucksack and told them to sit in a circle and turned on the music.

While the children enjoyed their last game, Vicky and Danielle put seven candles on the birthday cake. 'Pass the Parcel' was soon over and the lucky winner was Thea, the youngest of the party guests, who cuddled her prize, which was a lovely soft toy Labrador puppy.

Maya jumped up and cried, "How lovely, Thea loves dogs!"

With the candles lit, the birthday cake was brought out and everyone sang, "Happy birthday to you, happy birthday to you, happy birthday dear Sarah, happy birthday to you." When Sarah had blown out the candles and made a wish everyone clapped and agreed it had been a lovely party.

9. An Exciting End to a Perfect Day!

It was time for the guests to leave, but not before everyone was given a piece of birthday cake and a balloon to take home. Sarah hugged her school friends and said she was looking forward to seeing them next term.

With tears in her eyes she cuddled her Grandparents and wished them a safe journey home to Devon. Then Grandad Brian put his arms round her and promised to see her again very soon.

No-one wanted the party to end but, just as the guests prepared to leave, there was a shout from someone running towards them from the direction of the campsite office waving an envelope. It was the nice lady Sarah had met when she handed in the ring.

Breathlessly, the lady said, "Sarah, someone has claimed the ring and she was so grateful for your honesty that she left you this," and handed the envelope to Sarah.

Inside was a note that said, *'Please accept this gift with my enormous gratitude for finding my precious engagement ring. Best Wishes from Sophie.'*

Sarah gasped as she found the envelope also contained fifty pounds!

Everyone cheered, "Hip, hip, hooray for Sarah," and the party guests made their way to the entrance of the campsite, waving as they went home.

"Why didn't you tell me about the ring?" exclaimed Jennifer."

"I'm sorry, I forgot with everything else going on but, guess what, I'm going to treat my best friend to a new sparkly T-shirt!"

When everyone had gone, the two families gathered together and all agreed it had been a wonderful day, full of laughter and lots of fun – with the dramatic event of a collapsing tent thrown in!!

The End

CPSIA information can be obtained
at www.ICGtesting.com
Printed in the USA
LVHW070758240522
719534LV00009B/139